Watch William Walk

by Ann Jonas

For Wilma

Watercolor paints and a black pen were used
for the full-color art. The text type is Berthold
Akzidenz Grotesk.

Printed in Singapore by Tien Wah Press.
First Edition 10 9 8 7 6 5 4 3 2 1

Library of Congress Cataloging-in-Publication Data
Jonas, Ann.
Watch William walk / by Ann Jonas.
    p.   cm.
Summary: In this alliterative story, William and Wilma
take a walk with Wally the dog and Wanda the duck.
ISBN 0-688-14172-2 (trade)
ISBN 0-688-14175-7 (lib. bdg.)
[1. Walking—Fiction.   2. Dogs—Fiction.
3. Ducks—Fiction.]   I. Title.
PZ7.J664Wat   1997   [E]—dc20
96-7467   CIP   AC

Greenwillow Books, New York

Watch William walk with Wally.

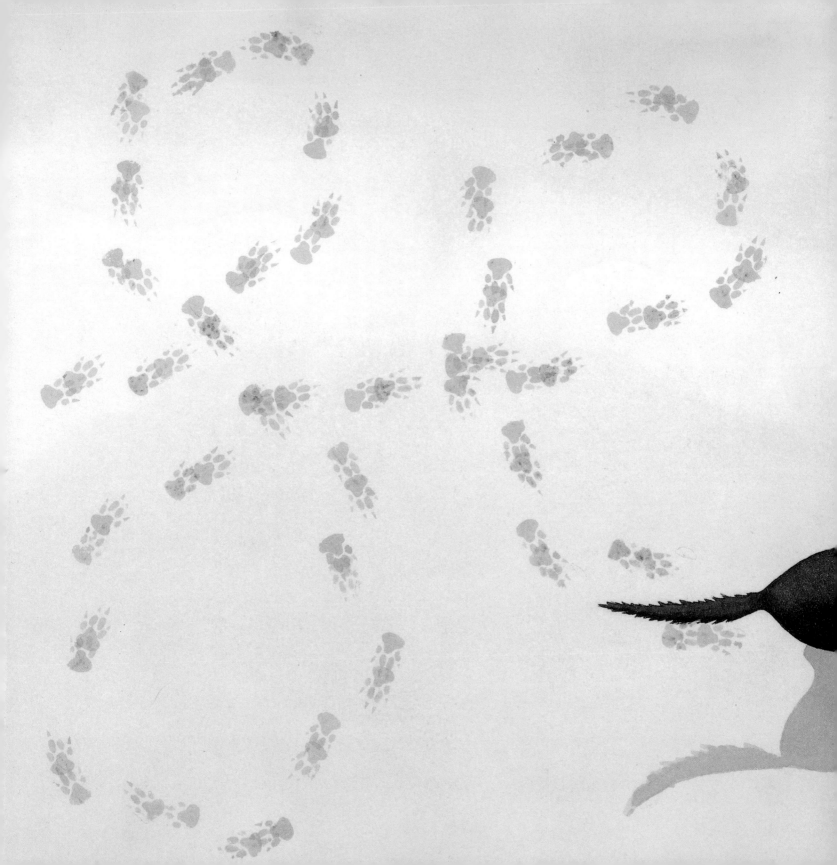

Wally welcomes
William's walks.
Wally wiggles.

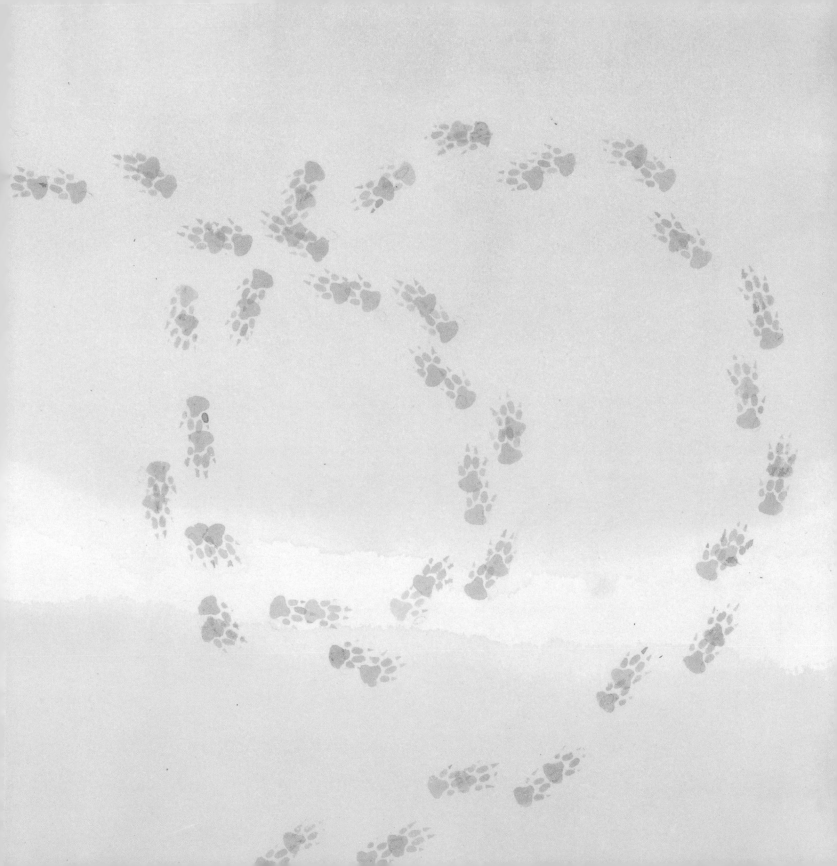

**William
waits
while
Wally
wanders.**

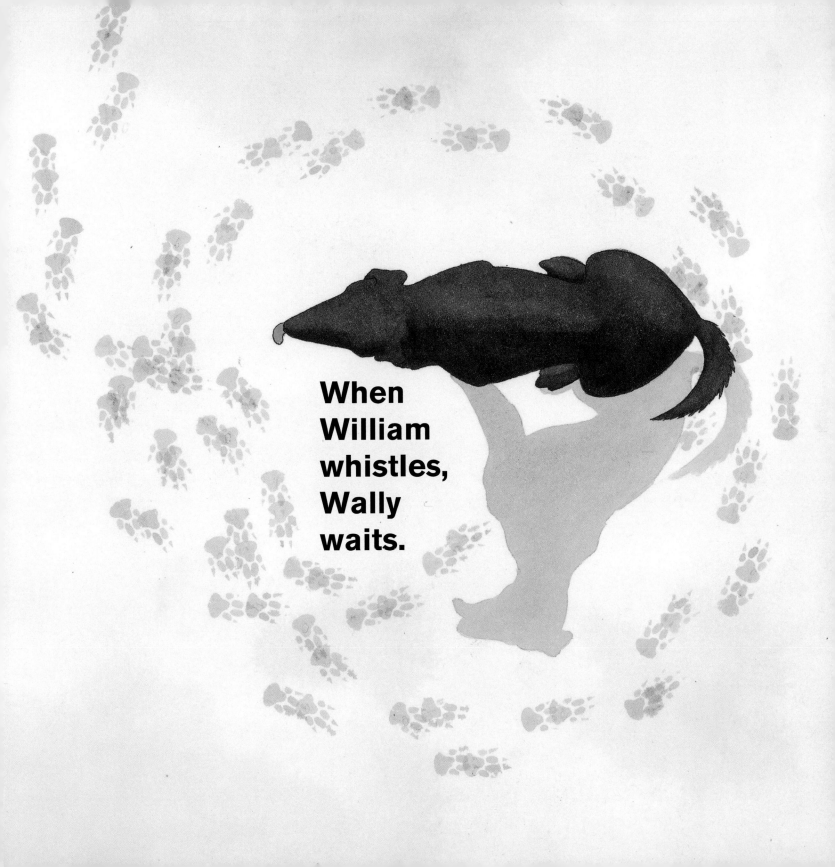

When
William
whistles,
Wally
waits.

Watch   **Wilma**

walk   with

Wanda.

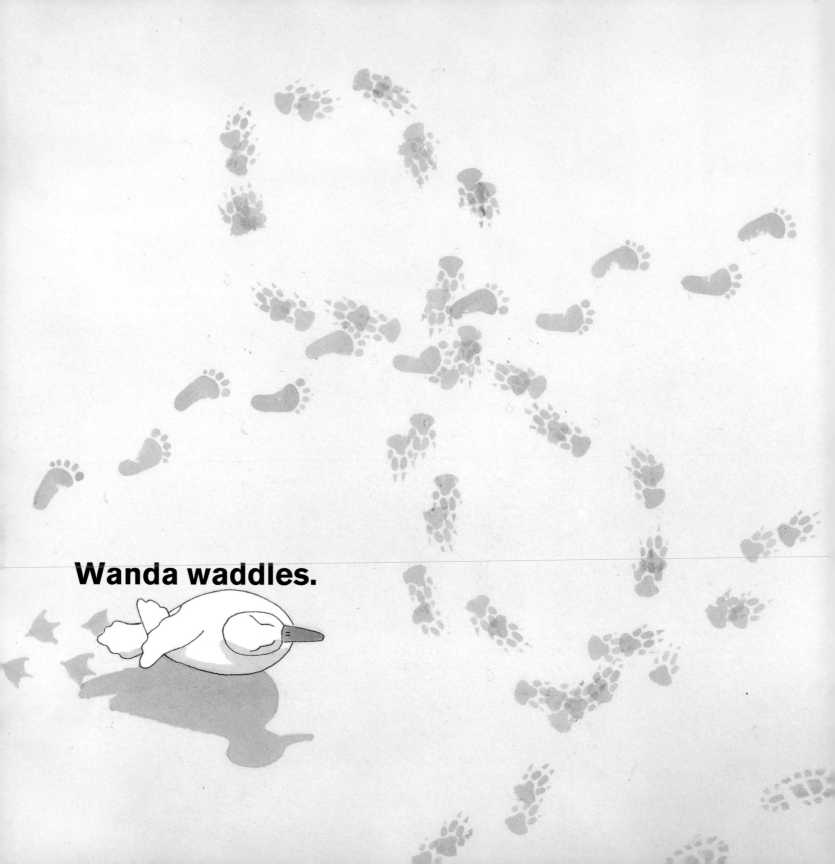

Wanda waddles.

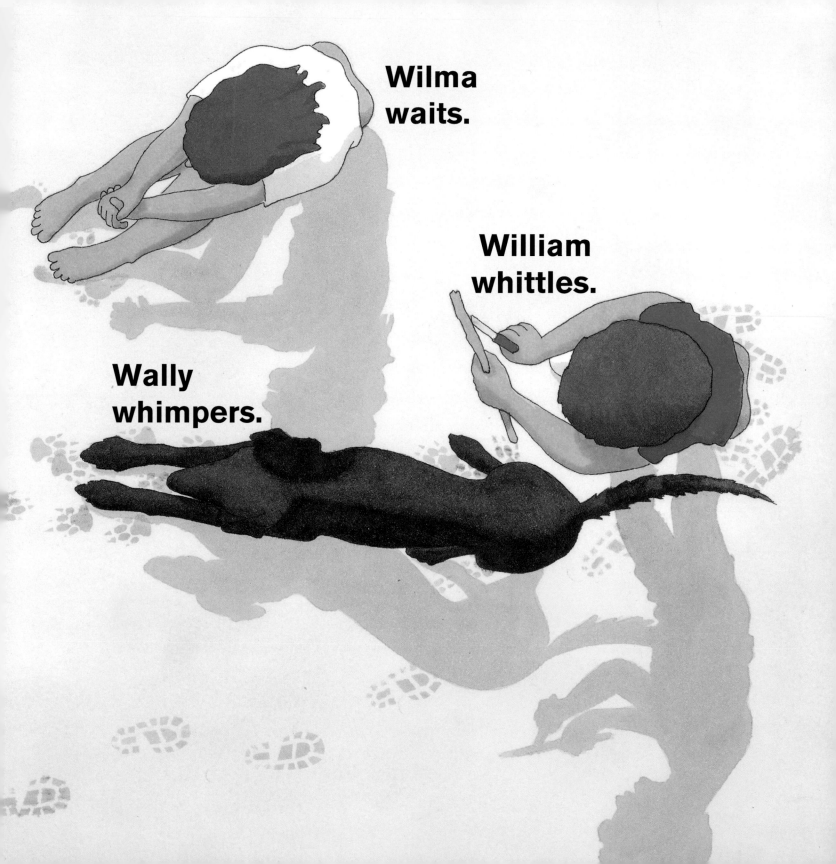

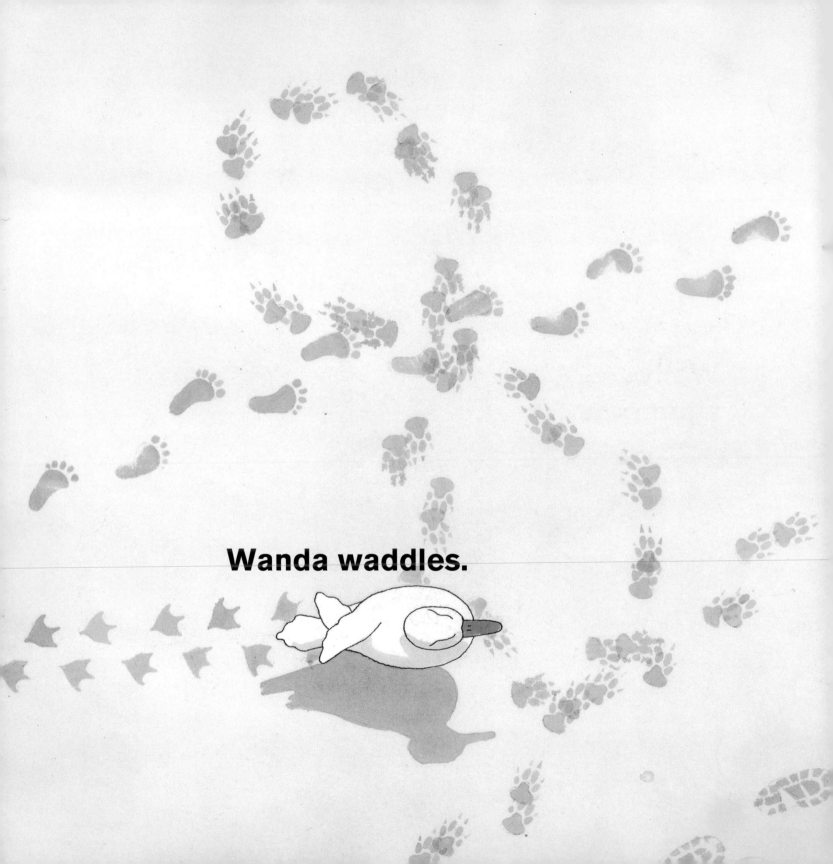

Wanda waddles.

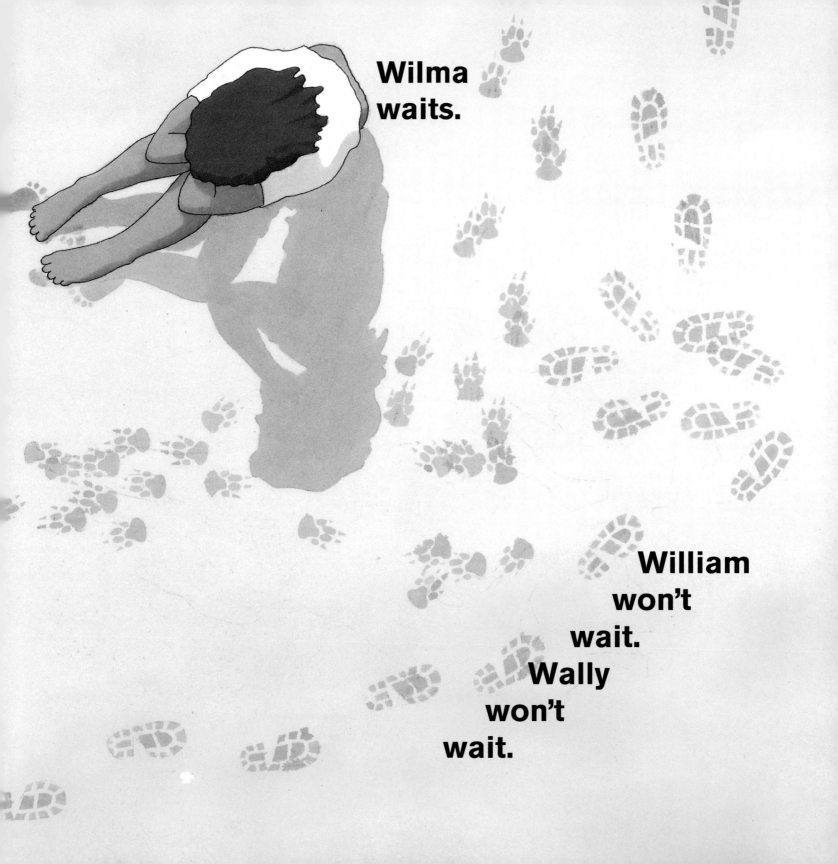

Wilma
waits.

William
won't
wait.
Wally
won't
wait.

William won't walk
with Wilma when
Wilma walks Wanda.

Wilma waves.

Wanda whiffs wetlands.

Water!

Wanda's wet.

Wanda wallows.

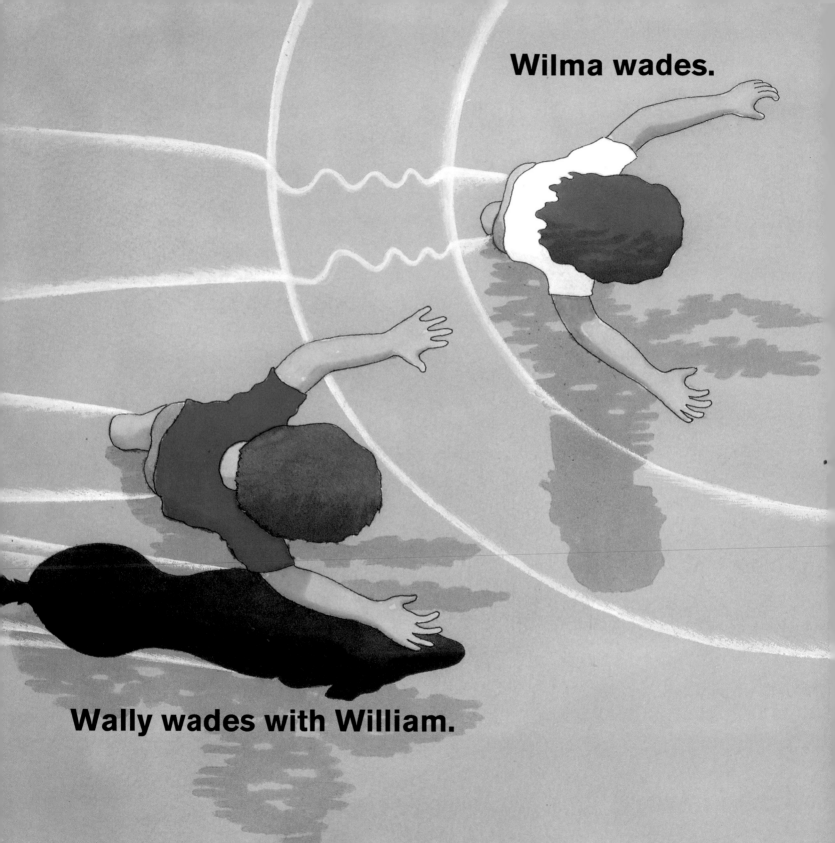

Wilma wades.

Wally wades with William.

Wilma's
weary.

William's
winded.

Wally
weakens.

Wanda's webfeet whirl.
Wanda's wake widens.

Waves! Whirlpools! Whitecaps!

When Wilma walks where water wets Wanda,
William will walk with Wilma.
Wally will walk with Wilma.

Wanda

won't

wait!